W16

SOUTHERN
OKLAHOMA
Library System
Ardmore, Oklahoma

D0325731

Betsy Ross
and the Silver Thimble

written by
Stephanie Greene

illustrated by
Diana Magnuson

Ready-to-Read
Aladdin

New York   London   T

**To my children,
Joshua and Samantha,
who bring us joy and light
—D.M.**

First Aladdin Edition June 2002
Text copyright © 2002 by Stephanie Greene
Illustrations copyright © 2002 by Diana Magnuson

Aladdin Paperbacks
An imprint of Simon & Schuster Children's Publishing Division
1230 Avenue of the Americas   New York, NY 10020

The text for this book was set in 17 Point Utopia
Designed by Lisa Vega
The illustrations were rendered in acrylic
Printed and bound in the United States of America
10 9 8 7 6 5 4 3 2 1

Greene, Stephanie.
Betsy Ross and the silver thimble / written by Stephanie Greene ; illustrated by Diana
Magnuson.— 1st. Aladdin Paperbacks ed.

p. cm. — (Ready-to-read)
Summary: Young Betsy Ross is upset when her brother tells her that she cannot make furniture
because she is a girl, but her mother teaches her that she can still do important things.
ISBN 0-689-84967-2 —ISBN 0-689-84954-0 (pbk.)
1. Ross, Betsy, 1752-1836—Childhood and youth—Juvenile literature. 2. Revolutionaries—
United States—Biography—Juvenile literature. 3. Women tailors—Pennsylvania—
Philadelphia—Biography—Juvenile literature. 4. Silver thimbles—Juvenile literature.
[1. Ross, Betsy, 1752-1836—Childhood and youth. 2. Revolutionaries. 3. Flags—United States.
4. Women—Biography.] I. Magnuson, Diana, ill. II. Title. III. Series.
E302.6.R77 G74 2002
973.3'092—dc21
[B]
ISBN 0-689-84954-0 (Aladdin pbk.)
ISBN 0-689-84967-2 (Aladdin Library Edition)

Betsy Ross
and the Silver Thimble

Little Betsy looked around
the dinner table.
There were her mother and father,
her six sisters, her brother, George.
Her two baby sisters were in bed.
"We have no more room
at this table," she said.

"Father is the best builder in town,"
said George.

"He can build a new table.
I will help."

"I will help, too," said Betsy.

"You can't make furniture," George said.

"You're a girl."

That made Betsy mad!

"You love to sew, Betsy,"
said her mother.
"Come sew with me."
But Betsy wanted to show George!

After dinner, Betsy went into
her father's workshop.
"I can make anything I want,"
she said.
"Like a table for my doll."

She looked at her father's tools.

She saw a big saw

hanging on the wall.

Betsy was glad George wasn't there.

She wanted to build a table

all by herself.

When she tried to take the saw down,
it hit her on the head.
"Ow!" cried Betsy.
But she wasn't going to
let a little bump stop her.

Betsy took some wood from the woodpile
and tried to cut it.

She tugged and pulled on the saw.

She sawed for a long time.

It was no fun at all.

Then all of a sudden—*zing!*—
the saw jumped from the board.
It cut Betsy's finger!

"Look, Mother!" Betsy cried
as she ran into the house.
"You could have been hurt very badly!"
said her mother.
"You do not know
how to use Father's tools.
A saw is not for a little girl."

"It's not fair!" Betsy cried.

"Little girls can't do anything."

"Betsy, do you really want
to make furniture?"
her mother asked.

Betsy thought about that old saw.

She did not like it one bit!

She only wanted to use it

because George said she couldn't.

"I want to give you something,"
said her mother.

"Hold out your hands
and close your eyes."

Betsy opened her eyes.
There on her finger was
a silver thimble.
"Oh, Mother," she cried.
"It's beautiful!"
"My mother gave it to me
when I was six years old,
just like you,"
her mother said.

"Now, look at your hands," said her mother.

"They are like two different people."

"What do you mean?" asked Betsy.

"Your left hand is you,

when you do things just because

someone else does them,"

her mother explained.

Betsy looked at her left hand.

It had a bandage on one finger.

Her finger hurt.

"Your right hand is you,
when you are being yourself."
When Betsy wiggled
her right hand,
the thimble swung
back and forth
like a little silver bell.
Her mother smiled.

"I *am* glad to be me," said Betsy.

Betsy remembered this lesson
her whole life.
She was proud to be a girl
who was true to herself.

*Betsy Ross sewed
for the rest of her life
and won many prizes.
Sewing turned out to be
very important—when Betsy Ross
grew up, she designed
our country's first flag.*

Here is a timeline of Betsy's life:

1752	Born in Philadelphia on January 1
1759	Goes to school for the first time
1763	Changes to the Quaker Friends School
1764	At age twelve, Betsy's school days are over
1765	Starts as an apprentice at John Webster's Upholstery Shop
1773	Marries John Ross
1776	John Ross dies
1776	In May, meets with George Washington to discuss the design of the flag. The flag is finished by early June.
1777	Marries Joseph Ashburn. Later, they have two daughters.
1782	Joseph Ashburn dies
1783	Marries John Claypoole in May. Later, they have five daughters.
1817	John Claypoole dies
1836	Dies peacefully on January 30 at eighty-four